Head for Trouble!

*Look out for more stories
about this spooky family!*

Haunted Treasure!

Head for Trouble!

Frank Rodgers

SCHOLASTIC

Scholastic Children's Books,
Commonwealth House, 1-19 New Oxford Street,
London, WC1A 1NU, UK
a division of Scholastic Ltd
London ~ New York ~ Toronto ~ Sydney ~ Auckland
Mexico City ~ New Delhi ~ Hong Kong

First published by Scholastic Ltd, 2002

Text and illustrations copyright © Frank Rodgers, 2002

ISBN 0 439 99451 9

Printed and bound by Cox and Wyman Ltd, Reading, Berks

2 4 6 8 10 9 7 5 3 1

Chapter One

Charlie Chill looked up at the big plastic monsters and ghosts on the back wall of the Ghost Train.

"Let's see," he murmured to himself, "what did Aunt Jill say was the new combination?" He scratched his head and thought hard. "Oh, yes," he said suddenly. "Now I remember."

Reaching up, he
poked a monster's
eye twice then stuck
his finger up a
ghost's nose.

Silently a hidden door swung open and
Charlie slipped through into the darkness.

As usual, Charlie felt a rush of excitement.
He loved visiting his relatives, the Ghost
Train Chills, though they were the strangest
relatives anyone ever had. His Aunt Jill was
a vampire, Uncle Thothage was a mummy,
Cousin Bogle was a troll and Great Grandpa
McGill was a skeleton.

Charlie's parents tried hard to ignore them.
They called the Chills their "dreadful secret".

They were terrified that someone would find out they were related to such weird people. They hardly ever talked about the Chills and never visited them.

Charlie hurried along the cobwebby tunnel. On either side of him he could just make out the dark shapes of caves, coffins and a crawling creature or two. At the end of the tunnel was another door and beside it a tiny, dusty window. He peered through it to see who was at home. They were all there, sitting round the kitchen table.

His Aunt Jill, the owner of the Ghost Train, was busy putting McGill's head back on his shoulders. Charlie grinned. McGill was very fussy about his appearance. His tartan scarf was always neatly tied and his tailcoat freshly brushed, but he was always losing his head. Bogle and Thothage were doing their favourite things. Big, hairy, untidy Bogle was greedily eating cold, lumpy custard, and Thothage was sound asleep, his head on his arms, snoring.

Thothage was always complaining that he had been out of his nice cosy tomb for a hundred years and needed to catch up on his snoozing. There was a sprinkling of fine sand on the table that had drifted down from the wrinkles in his dusty wrapping.

Jill fixed McGill's head on at last and stood back to admire her handiwork, running her fingers through her towering purple hairdo.

Charlie smiled. He pressed the bell on the wall beside the door and waited.

Chapter Two

An ear-splitting scream tore round the Ghost Train kitchen.

AIIIEEEEE!

Thothage jerked his head up from the table and blinked.

"Nice tune, Jill," he muttered blearily.

"That wasn't me," replied Jill. "It was the doorbell."

She opened the door
and smiled in delight.

"Charlie!" she cried.
"Give your aunt
a big hug!"

"Hello, Aunt
Jill," said Charlie.
Jill squeezed
him tight then led
him into the low,
cobwebby kitchen.

"Look who's here!" she cried.

"Hello, Charlie!" cried the three other
Chills, beaming.

"It's lovely to see you again," gushed Jill.
"How's school?"

"Well," he said slowly. "That's why I'm
here, Aunt. I need your advice. Something's
happened at school."

"Aha!" Jill cried in delight. "You've been
expelled at last! How lovely! Congratulations!"

"No, it's not that, Aunt," said Charlie.

"Did you let off some nice rotten stink-bombs in the classroom, laddie?" asked McGill eagerly.

"No ... not that either."

"Did you scare the teacher the way I showed you?" asked Bogle, pulling his big face out of shape like a piece of putty.

"Yeeuurgh! No!"

"Did you put an ancient Egyptian curse on the school like I taught you?" murmured Thothage.

"No chance," responded Charlie again.

The Chills looked at each other, puzzled.

"What then?" they cried together.

"The school's going to have to sell its sports field," said Charlie, looking glum.

The Chills stared at Charlie blankly.

"What's wrong with that?" they said.

"No more football," replied Charlie. "No

more rugby or rounders ... no more school sports ... no more races."

Thothage yawned.

"Races?" he mumbled. "Too tiring."

"Oh, no!" cried McGill excitedly, his head bouncing up and down on his bony shoulders. "Races are grand. Good for the legs!"

He began to wiggle the first two fingers of each hand on the table like legs running.

"I remember when I was a wee sporty laddie in..."

Suddenly McGill's hands jumped out of his sleeves and began to race each other round the table.

"Hey! Come back here, you two!" yelled McGill.

Jill and Charlie both made an attempt to grab them but they were too slow. Round and round the table sprinted the five-fingered flyers.

The table-top was like an obstacle course and the hands leaped over empty dishes and slid on trails of custard until Bogle suddenly dropped one of his huge arms in front of them. The hands tripped over the outstretched limb and flew into the air, turning over and over. McGill stretched up and caught them expertly in his empty sleeves.

"Aha!" he cried, wiggling his fingers triumphantly. "Got you! Now behave yourselves, you silly wee runaway digits!"

Jill turned to Charlie.

"But why would your school want to sell the sports field?" she asked.

"They don't want to," replied Charlie. "But they need the money. The safe in the Head Teacher's study was opened and an envelope full of cash was stolen. It was the money we raised from the fête last weekend. The school needs it urgently to buy books and computers."

"Are there any suspects?" asked Bogle.

"Not at the moment," said Charlie.

The Chills all scratched their heads.

"So how can we help?" asked his aunt. "You said you wanted our advice."

Charlie nodded. "Yes," he replied. "You see, Brat Gripewater, the millionaire builder, was at the school earlier today. I recognized him from the papers. He was there with two men and they all looked very pleased with themselves. There's a rumour going round that he's offered to help the school by buying the playing field. I remembered you saying once that Brat Gripewater was a twister, so I came to find out what you meant."

"Brat Gripewater?" snarled McGill. "Of course he's a twister! I wouldn't trust him if I were your Head Teacher!"

The other Chills nodded in agreement.

"He's power-mad, Charlie," explained his Aunt Jill. "Wants to buy up the whole town. He and his two slimy cronies, Lance Boyle and Slinky Eels, tried to cheat me out of the Ghost Train recently – that's why I know he's a bad lot. Your Head Teacher had better be very careful if she's dealing with him!"

Charlie nodded. "Boyle and Eels must have been the two men with Brat at school. Thanks, Aunt. I'll have to warn Ms Binns. If only we could find out who stole the money and get it back ... then we wouldn't have to sell the playing field."

"Don't you worry, laddie," said McGill confidently. "Your great grandpa will find out. I've always fancied myself as a detective."

"And we'll help too!" exclaimed Jill.

"Er ... how?" asked Charlie anxiously.

His aunt beamed. "It just came to me. We'll give a concert at the school to raise money!"

"What?" gasped Charlie in shock. "A concert? At my school? B-b-but you can't come to my school. It would be..."

"Fabulous!" cried Jill, brimming with excitement.

"But Aunt Jill," protested Charlie. "You're not... I mean, you don't look..."

"Normal?" said his aunt, with a twinkle in her eye. "I know. But don't worry. Everyone will just think we're dressed up like entertainers. And we won't use our real names. No one will know we're related!"

She turned to the others.

"I'll sing some songs ... Thothage can perform some magic ... McGill can play the accordion and Bogle can do a strong man act. It'll be a sensation! The school will make a fortune and your problem will be solved!"

"But…" protested Charlie weakly.

"No need to thank me, my boy," retorted Jill, grinning. "I'll phone your Head Teacher in the morning and tell her all about it. And remember," she went on, winking, "not a word to your mum and dad. If they find out it's us they'll go into orbit!"

Chapter Three

The next morning Charlie rushed to school early. He was desperate to put a stop to his aunt's mad idea. His only hope was to try and persuade Ms Binns to say no when his aunt phoned. He also wanted to warn her about Brat Gripewater. But he was too late. Brat's car was already outside with Lance and Slinky lounging beside it ... and Brat was in Ms Binns's office.

Charlie groaned in frustration. He slumped against the wall of the corridor, wondering what to do. Just then the Head Teacher's door opened and he heard Brat's smooth, oily voice.

"Of course," he was saying, "after I've bought the playing field I'll only put up a couple of teensy buildings. You'll hardly even know they're there! I'll bring the documents for your signature in a few days."

Charlie gasped. So that's what was going on! Brat was planning to build on the playing field!

"But I still haven't decided, Mr Gripewater..." Ms Binns replied.

At that moment Lance Boyle came along the corridor. Charlie turned away from the door and studied the noticeboard, trying to look innocent. Lance ignored him.

"Bye then, Ms Binns," said Brat, appearing in the open doorway. "See you soon."

He closed the door behind him.

"Call for you on your mobile, boss," said Lance.

"Right," replied Brat and suddenly noticed Charlie. He leaned forward with a smirk on his face. "I know what you'd like to be when you grow up, sonny," he said.

Charlie glared at him.

"Do you?"

"Yeah. As rich as me!" replied Brat, and snorted with laughter.

"Nice one, boss," said Lance with a toadying laugh as they walked away. "Nice one!"

"Yes, I'm quite a wit, me," said Brat smugly.

Charlie gazed after them angrily. He had to tell Ms Binns that Brat was not to be trusted. Without stopping to think he rushed into the Head Teacher's room and gasped out, "Ms Binns! Ms Binns! You mustn't sell the sports field to Brat Gripewater. You mustn't! He's up to no good. My Aunt Jill says so."

"Your Aunt Jill? What has she got to do with it?" said Ms Binns, confused. "Anyway, I haven't signed Brat's ... er ... Mr Gripewater's contract yet. And what's more," she said, suddenly glaring at Charlie, "how did you know he had offered to buy the sports field?"

As Charlie struggled to think of a reason he was saved by the ringing of the telephone.

Ms Binns reached for it, still keeping a beady eye on Charlie.

"Ms Binns, Head Teacher," she sang and then listened intently to the caller.

Charlie's head was so full of possible excuses for his eavesdropping that he completely forgot why he was there. It was only when Ms Binns put the phone down that he came to his senses.

"The phone!" he cried wildly. "Er ... the phone call, Ms Binns. Who was it?"

"I beg your pardon?" said Ms Binns frostily.

"I mean, was it my Aunt Jill?"

"There you go again with your Aunt Jill," said Ms Binns. "As a matter of fact it wasn't your Aunt Jill..."

"Oh, good..." Charlie sighed with relief.

"...it was the world famous opera singer Madame Screechowtski. I can't say I've ever heard of her, but then I don't know much about opera. She has very kindly offered to put on a concert to help us raise funds for the school. It seems that someone told her of our plight. And she is going to bring along some other world-famous acts: Pharaoh McFakery, the magician; Fingers O'Bone, the accordion player; and Mr Muscle Mountain, the strongest man in the world."

"Oh, no!" groaned Charlie to himself.

"Won't that be marvellous?" said Ms Binns. "We might not have to sell the sports field after all."

26

Chapter Four

That evening Charlie hurried to see the Chills. "I've got news!" he cried. "Brat Gripewater does want to buy the school playing field! But he's promised only to build on part of it and leave the rest to the school!"

The Chills gasped.

"Your Head Teacher doesn't really believe that, does she?" asked Jill anxiously. "Surely she hasn't signed anything?"

"She's going to wait until after the concert," replied Charlie. "To see if we make enough money."

"Very sensible," murmured Thothage, waking up.

Charlie winced.

"Er ... can't you think of another way to make money?" he asked nervously. "Please? Without coming to my school?"

"Oh, don't you worry," answered his aunt, beaming. "It'll be fine."

"Brat Gripewater's up to something," said McGill, frowning fiercely. "There's more to this playing-field business than meets the eye. And I'd like to bet that he had something to do with the school fête money going missing. But how can we find out?"

Jill snapped her fingers. "I know what to do!" she cried. "We'll go and investigate Gripewater's office!"

"Good thinking!" exclaimed McGill. "We're sure to find out what he's up to in there!"

"You can't do that!" gasped Charlie, aghast. "It's against the law!"

"It's not against the law if Bogle happens to lean on a door and it falls in, is it?" asked Jill innocently.

"And while we're there helping him up we might just happen to find some proof that Gripewater is a twister," McGill went on.

"But..." protested Charlie.

"Don't worry, Charlie," said his aunt once again. "It'll be fine."

Brat's headquarters were on the ground floor of a big, shiny, new office block in a side street. The building was closed and the lights were off.

"Nobody in," said Jill, peering in through the window as Charlie and the others gathered round.

"Can I lean on the door now?" asked Bogle happily.

Jill looked around.

"Better not, Bogle," she said. "There are people nearby and it would make too much noise."

"But how are we goin' to get in?" Bogle said, disappointed.

Jill pointed to a gap under the door. "Through there," she said.

Bogle studied the gap. "I think I'm too big."

"Not you, Bogle," said Jill. "Thothage."

"Eh?" said Thothage, who had been trying to fall asleep against the wall. "What? Me?"

"Yes, you," answered Jill. "You can transform yourself into something really small, creep inside and find out what Brat's plans are."

Thothage yawned.
"Do I have
to?" he said.
"Transformations
are so tiring."

"Yes, you do
have to!" snapped
Jill impatiently.
"Now hurry up. We haven't got all day.
We're due back in the tunnel shortly."

Thothage sighed and rubbed his eyes.

"Oh, well," he said. "If I must."

He closed his eyes, stretched out his arms
and began to chant.

> Akhenaton, Nefertiti,
> Ka, Ka, Ka.
> Thoth, Anubis, Ptah and Seti,
> Ra, Ra, Ra!

There was a bright flash and suddenly
everyone was enveloped in a cloud of
orange smoke. When the smoke cleared
they saw that Thothage had disappeared.

"Where did he go?" asked a bewildered Bogle.

"There," said Charlie, pointing.

Everyone looked down and there by the door, yawning and rubbing its eyes, was a tiny mouse.

"Go for it, wee Thothage!" cried McGill in delight.

The mouse looked up, sighed, yawned again and slowly crawled under the door.

"I hope he doesn't fall asleep on the job," muttered Jill, looking through the glass again.

They all peered in through the window.
"There he is!" cried Charlie. "On the desk!"
"He's reading a sheet of paper," said Jill,
excitedly. "Could be important."

"There's something else on the desk too,"
muttered McGill, straining to see. "And it's
moving."
Suddenly everyone shouted out at the
same time. "It's a cat! Thothage!" they
yelled. "Look out! There's a cat behind
you!"

Thothage's sleepy eyes flew open and, dropping the paper, he leaped from the desk. Just in time.

Sharp claws tore the air and a black, hissing streak of fur leaped after him.

"Run!" cried Charlie.

In panic Thothage dodged this way and that, trying to avoid the claws of the sooty assassin. But no matter where he ran the black cat was always right behind him.

At last, in desperation, Thothage ran up the curtains.

The cat followed, but halfway up its claws got tangled in the material. It was stuck ... for the moment.

"Now's your chance!" yelled McGill.

Thothage jumped.

He bounced off the startled cat as if it were a furry trampoline. Landing safely on the floor he took to his heels and scampered across the room.

Two seconds later the mouse emerged, panting, from under the door.

"Oh, thank goodness you're safe!" cried Jill, patting the little head.

Thothage wiped his mousey brow. "Never again!" he said in a tiny voice and squeaked out another chant.

Everybody blinked as the mouse disappeared in a bright blue flash and a huge puff of purple smoke.

When the smoke cleared there was Thothage, leaning against the wall, yawning loudly.

"Did you find anything out, Thothage?" asked Jill excitedly.

"Mmmm?" muttered Thothage sleepily.

"What was on the piece of paper you were reading?" Jill went on.

"Plans," replied Thothage in a tired voice. "Of the school playing field."

"What was on the plans, ancient Egyptian laddie?" asked McGill tetchily.

"Buildings," said Thothage. "The playing field was full of houses, offices and car parks. No space left for anything else."

"I knew it!" exclaimed Charlie. "Brat Gripewater is a twister! He said there would be space left over for a sports field and there isn't. I must tell Ms Binns!"

Chapter Five

There was no reply when Charlie knocked on the Head Teacher's door next morning.

"Looking for Ms Binns, are you, Charlie?" asked Mrs Pratt, the school secretary, coming out of her office. "You're out of luck, I'm afraid. She's gone."

"When will she be back?" asked Charlie anxiously.

"Tomorrow evening, just before the concert," replied Mrs Pratt. "She's at a conference." She grinned cheerily. "We're all really excited about the concert. Ms Binns even phoned the local radio station about it before she left. We're sure to get a big crowd tomorrow!"

Charlie groaned to himself in disappointment. He would have to wait until tomorrow to tell Ms Binns about Brat's nasty intentions.

🐾 🐾 🐾

Brat Gripewater heard about the concert on the radio later that morning and flew into a rage.

"This will ruin my plans!" he bawled. "If the school makes enough money from the concert then Ms Binns won't sell me the playing field! We need a plan!" He glared at Lance and Slinky. "Think!" he shouted. "Think!"

"Er ... maybe we could sneak in tonight and blow up the school?" suggested Slinky.

Brat ground his teeth. "A bit drastic, don't you think?" He looked at them pityingly. "As usual, I'll have to come up with the idea."

Lance and Slinky nodded their heads.

"That would be best, boss," they said.

🐾 🐾 🐾

That evening Charlie got another unpleasant surprise. His mum and dad had heard about the concert, too, and had decided to go. In vain he tried to persuade them not to.

"Oh, you couldn't keep me away," said his mum with a grin. "I'm looking forward to seeing Mr Muscle Mountain. He sounds dishy!"

"And I can't wait to hear Madame Screetchowtski's wonderful singing," said his dad.

Charlie began to panic. Everything seemed to be out of control. He couldn't tell his parents the truth because he had promised not to. His only hope was that a miracle might happen and the concert would be cancelled. If not then he and the Chills were heading for trouble!

A miracle didn't happen and next evening, with a sinking heart, Charlie secretly guided his weird relations to the school. Because he used the side streets only a handful of people saw the Chills.

As these passers-by stopped and stared, mouths hanging open, Charlie was able to call out quite truthfully, "It's the school concert party..." and they immediately relaxed and waved cheerily.

The back door of the school was open and Charlie managed to get his relatives inside without being spotted by anyone. He ushered the Chills along the empty corridors and into the room behind the stage.

"Now, stay put everyone, OK?" Charlie said. "I'll go and tell Ms Binns you're here."

A few moments after Charlie had left, McGill slapped his forehead and gasped.

"My accordion!" he wailed. "I left it behind! I'll have to go home and get it!"

Before anyone could argue he dashed out of the door.

"Don't be long!" yelled Jill.

"Don't worry, he's a fast mover is old skelly-bones," said Bogle in admiration.

"Too fast," muttered Thothage, stifling a yawn. "All that speed makes me tired. I think I'll have a short nap before the performance."

He looked around but couldn't see anywhere to lie down. "I'll find somewhere else," he muttered under his breath and when Jill and Bogle weren't looking he slipped out of the door.

In the hall Ms Binns was busy greeting everyone.

"Oh, hello, Charlie," she gushed. "It looks like our concert is going to be a terrific success. The takings for this evening should certainly make up for the missing money. Won't that be wonderful?!"

Charlie nodded. "It certainly will, Ms Binns," he agreed, "because I've come across some important information about Mr Gripewater."

Ms Binns looked sharply at Charlie.
"What information?"

"Well," replied Charlie, "I was with my
Aunt Jill, and..."

Ms Binns' eyes narrowed.

"Your Aunt Jill again, Charlie. I'll have to
meet this lady." She peered at him. "Well,
what about her?"

"We found out that Mr Gripewater intends
to build over all of the sports field and leave
the school nothing."

Ms Binns looked shocked.

"Have you and your aunt any proof?"

"Well ... no," Charlie admitted. He could hardly tell Ms Binns that his uncle had found out by turning into a mouse and breaking into Brat's office. "But it's true."

Ms Binns nodded her head slowly.

"It may well be, Charlie," she said, "but I'll have to see some proof."

She looked at her watch and gasped. "It's almost time for the concert to begin! Where are Madame Screetchowtski and the others? I hope they're not late!"

"It's all right," Charlie said quickly. "They're here already. I escorted them to the room behind the stage. That's what I came to tell you."

The Head Teacher beamed.

"Well done, Charlie," she said. "Now, run along and tell them that Madame is on first and that I will introduce her."

Charlie groaned inwardly and turned away.

Just then his mum and dad came into the hall.

"Is she here, Charlie?" asked his dad eagerly. "Have you seen Madame Screetchowtski? What does she look like?"

Charlie sighed. There was no getting out of it now. It was obvious ... he would have to tell his parents the truth.

Taking them aside he whispered, "Er, actually ... she looks like Aunt Jill."

His dad stared at him blankly. "What do you mean?" he said nervously.

"What I mean," replied Charlie slowly, "is ... that it isn't Madame Screetchowtski ... it's Aunt Jill ... and the others."

Charlie's parents turned pale.

"The Ghost Train Chills...." muttered his dad hoarsely. "The family's dreadful secret. I might have known it would get out sooner or later." He looked around the hall furtively, as if he expected to see all the parents whispering about it.

"Everyone thinks they're just performers, Dad," said Charlie. "Nobody knows who they really are."

"Let's hope it stays that way," said his mum.

"Why didn't you try to stop them, Charlie?" hissed his dad.

"I did," whispered Charlie. "But you know how forceful Aunt Jill can be when she's got a bee in her bonnet."

"We know," his dad muttered mournfully. "We know."

Chapter Six

Thothage blinked at the putty-coloured walls
of the corridor as he shuffled along sleepily.

"Reminds me of the Tomb of Tutankhamun,"
he muttered, "but not as cosy." In a little
hallway off the corridor a bright blue door
with a rainbow painted on it attracted his
attention. Thothage opened it and
immediately saw what he was looking for.

"What a lovely place to sleep," he murmured, beaming. Crossing the room he stepped into the large sandpit and lay down. "Ahhhh," he sighed blissfully as he wriggled himself into the soft sand. "Perfect. So comfy. Just like home!" He closed his eyes and began to doze off.

At that moment he heard voices in the corridor right outside the door and was dimly aware that he recognized them.

"Hmmm," he murmured sleepily. "That's that slippery customer Brat Gripewater and his two cronies, Lance Boyle and Slinky Eels."

"Right, boss," Thothage heard Lance say. "Don't worry. We'll carry out your plan. We'll make sure the lights fail just before the concert."

"Yeah," said Slinky. "It'll be dead easy to find the main electricity circuit board and put it out of action. It's in the basement."

"Good," replied Brat and sniggered. "The concert will be a disaster and Ms Binns will come running to sign my document of sale."

"Pity the school money dodge didn't work," said Lance.

"It would have if those dratted performers hadn't got involved," said Brat darkly. He shrugged. "But never mind. It certainly fooled them, didn't it? They think their money's been stolen, but it hasn't. What would I want with hot cash? I'm not a common thief. If I'm going to be caught for something it's not going to be for stealing a piddly little School Fund."

"No," Lance went on with a snigger. "But you knew where to put it, didn't you?"

Brat laughed. "Certainly did, Lance," he said. "Certainly did. It's right under her nose in a very safe place." He laughed again. "A safe place, get it?"

"We do, boss, we do!" cried Lance and Slinky, snorting with laughter.

They walked away laughing as Thothage struggled to stay awake.

"Must tell the others..." he mumbled. "Must ... tell..." and with that he gave a great yawn and fell fast asleep.

McGill was lost. He had been blundering round the empty corridors for about ten minutes looking for the way out. He stopped and scratched his head. "All these corridors look the same!" he muttered. "How do the children ever find their way?" But just then he felt a cold gust of air on his face. He peered round a corner. There, at the end of the corridor was the back door, lying wide open.

"At last!" he cried and charged towards it.

Along the wall to his left was a double row of metal lockers. There were long ones at the bottom and shorter ones at the top. Just as McGill ran past them, one of the top locker doors swung open in the draught and connected suddenly with his head ... CLANG ... knocking it clean off his shoulders.

"What happened?" he cried as his head bounced once then began to roll back along the corridor.

The rest of McGill kept going. It ran straight through the open door and out into the playground where it stopped, confused.

Turning round twice, it began to blunder about with its arms outstretched, searching for its head. After a few tottering steps it reached the steps leading down to the basement. One foot stepped into mid-air and, with a kind of rushing stumble, the headless body toppled forward and staggered down the steps two at a time. At the foot of the stairs it flew through the open door and landed on its bottom with a thump.

Immediately McGill's hands leaped out of his sleeves and went racing across the floor looking for his head.

At the other end of the darkened basement, Lance and Slinky were searching for the main circuit board with torches. They hadn't heard McGill's spectacular entrance because of the gurgling and sighing sounds from the big boiler that sat in the middle of the room.

"Must be around here somewhere," complained Lance as they crept along.

A pattering noise near his feet made Slinky swing his torch down.

"Ah!" he yelped in fright as he saw something in the beam. "Lance! Look! Two of them!"

Lance pointed his torch in the same direction but by then there was nothing to be seen.

"Don't be such a scaredy-cat!" he snorted in disgust. "It was probably rats."

"No, Lance," cried Slinky, trembling. "It was hands! Honest! A pair of hands ... scuttling across the floor like big, bony spiders! Horrible!"

"Pull yourself together, Slinky!" commanded Lance. "Of course it was just rats. What else could it be?"

Away in the shadows behind the boilers McGill's hands had finished their tour of the basement and had jumped back into their sleeves.

The headless body got up from the floor and, arms outstretched once more, began to feel its way round the basement.

At the other end Lance had found some pipes and cables attached to the wall.

"Cables!" he crowed. "All we have to do is follow them." He and Slinky played their torch beams along them and a few seconds later Lance grinned. "Hey presto!"

There in front of them was a big panel full of meters and switches.

Lance took a hammer out of his pocket.

"Now for the bit I was looking forward to," he sniggered. "A bit of circuit breaking."

He raised his hammer, but at that moment a shuffling noise in the shadows made them both start nervously. They swung their torches round and there, caught in the glare, was an awful sight.

A headless figure was moving towards them, arms stetched out and fingers groping.

Two torches and a hammer dropped from limp fingers on to the stone floor with a clatter.

Lance and Slinky stood frozen to the spot with fear. Slinky's eyes boggled and Lance's mouth twitched.

"Ah..." they whimpered. "Ah...."

Suddenly they found their voices and their legs and ran screaming from the basement.

"AAAAAAAH!"

Bumping into the walls and falling over each other they scrambled up the steps and out into the playground.

Brat was waiting for them at the top of the stairs and Lance and Slinky nearly knocked him over.

"What's going on?" he cried.

"A g-g-g-ghost! A headless ghost!" yelled Lance.

"Run for your life!" screamed Slinky.

Without looking behind them once they tore wildly across the playground, out of the gate, around the corner and out of sight.

Brat Gritted his teeth.

His plan to sabotage the concert had failed.

Chapter Seven

Charlie watched anxiously from behind the curtain in the wings as his Aunt Jill swept majestically on to the stage. She had just been introduced by Ms Binns as "that truly great and shining star of the opera" and the audience were clapping loudly.

Jill held up her hands and the clapping stopped.

"Tonight," she proclaimed, "I am going to treat you to a selection from my favourite musicals."

Charlie groaned.

"But I will begin," Jill went on, "with that old favourite, Oklahoma..."

Charlie relaxed again, until Jill continued, "...sung to my own words."

"Madame Screetchowtski" threw out her arms, tossed her head back and opened her mouth. At first no sound came out, then gradually everyone heard a noise like a distant fire engine siren getting nearer and nearer ... *Traaaaaaaaaaaaaa* ... until, suddenly, it blasted out across the audience with a screaming, stunning force.

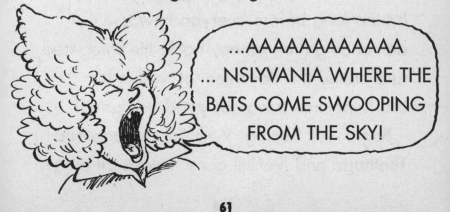

...AAAAAAAAAAAA ... NSLYVANIA WHERE THE BATS COME SWOOPING FROM THE SKY!

The audience was transfixed – shocked, wide-eyed and slack-jawed. They had never heard anything so awful in their lives.

At the back of the hall, once he got over his shock, Brat Gripewater smirked with satisfaction. It didn't matter that his plan to sabotage the concert had failed. With all this awful screeching going on it wouldn't be too long before everybody was demanding their money back. He sniggered and patted the document of sale in his inside pocket. It was as good as signed!

Bogle was fretting. With Jill on stage and Thothage and McGill gone he was all alone.

"I'm lonely, Charlie," moaned Bogle, appearing at Charlie's side. "I've no one to talk to and I haven't had a chance to practise my strong man act."

Charlie looked puzzled.

"Lonely?" he said. "But surely Thothage and Great Grandpa McGill are with you?"

Bogle shook his big, hairy head forlornly. "Nope," he replied. "Both gone."

"What!" yelped Charlie. "Where to?"

"Dunno," mumbled Bogle. "They just went."

As Charlie stood staring at Bogle in panic a faint rumbling sound made the pair look behind them. Rolling towards them down the corridor was McGill's head.

Before either of them could react it trundled right past them and on to the stage.

Jill had just finished her song and the audience were sitting stunned and silent. The head came to a rest at her feet and the silence was broken by a scream from the front row.

"It's a skull!"

"And it winked at me!" shrieked another voice.

Charlie rushed on to the stage and picked it up. Jill rolled her eyes and tutted. "It's not time for your act yet, Grandpa," she hissed.

McGill opened his mouth to reply but Charlie clapped his hand over it just in time. As he hurried offstage with the runaway head tucked under his arm he looked winningly at the front row.

"Er ... I hope you enjoy the rest of the concert?" he said.

But the front row had had enough ...

and so had the rest of the audience. They stood up and started to leave.

"I can't take any more," said one faintly.

"Nor me," said another.

"I want my money back," said someone else and everyone joined in.

"We want our money back!"

Frowning, Jill watched as the audience shuffled towards the back of the hall and a crestfallen Ms Binns.

"Hm!" sniffed Jill. "Some people just don't appreciate good music!"

She joined Charlie and Bogle at the side of the stage and peered into McGill's face.

"Where's the rest of you?" she demanded.

McGill wiggled his eyebrows towards the corridor.

"It went thataway," he said. "But I don't know where it is now."

Charlie groaned again. The concert had turned out to be as big a disaster as he had feared.

"We'll have to find it, Great Grandpa," he said. "Before someone else does! Come on!"

"What about Thothage?" Jill asked as they hurried along.

Charlie stopped in his tracks.

"I'd forgotten about him!" he wailed.

"Charlie, laddie," said McGill suddenly.

Charlie looked down at the head in his arms.

"Yes?"

"Do my old bony earholes deceive me or is that the sound of snoring I hear?"

Everyone listened.

Sure enough, just audible over the muttering of the audience in the hall was a familiar noise.

"It's Thothage!" cried Jill. "I'd know that snoring anywhere!"

"It's coming from in here," said Bogle, pushing open a door with a rainbow on it.

"He's in the sandpit!" exclaimed Charlie as they went into the nursery playroom. "What's he doing in there?"

"It probably reminds him of Egypt," said Jill fondly. "That's full of sand, you know."

They crossed the room and Bogle shook Thothage by the shoulder.

"Wakey wakey!" he bellowed into his ear.

Thothage jerked like a puppet and sat up, blinking and brushing sand out of his face.

"Wh-what's up?" he mumbled sleepily. "Is something the matter?"

Charlie raised his eyes and sighed.

"Oh, not a lot," he said. "Except for the concert being a complete disaster, everyone asking for their money back and McGill's body going missing." He sighed again. "Brat Gripewater has won after all."

Thothage yawned.

"Oh, yes," he said slowly. "I heard him talking to Slinky and Lance just before I fell asleep."

"What did he say?" asked Charlie.

"Well," mused Thothage, "they seemed quite pleased that everyone had assumed the school's money was stolen when it wasn't."

Charlie gasped. "The money wasn't stolen?"

"Apparently not," said Thothage.

Charlie looked blank.

"But if it wasn't stolen, where is it?"

Thothage mulled this over.

"Somewhere right under her nose, I think he said. In a safe place. A safe place. They thought this was hilarious and they laughed. I've no idea why. I don't think 'a safe place' is particularly funny, do you?"

"Right under her nose..." murmured Charlie.

"In a safe place..." muttered Jill.

They looked at each other.

"Safe..." repeated Charlie. "Aunt Jill, do you think..."

"I do think, Charlie. I do." She turned to Bogle and Thothage, who was clambering out of the sandpit. "Come on, you two!" she cried. "We're going to Ms Binns's office!"

As they ran out of the room they almost collided with the rest of McGill. It was stumbling along the corridor, arms flapping.

"There you are!" yelled McGill happily.

Jill quickly fitted McGill's head back on his shoulders. The delighted skeleton did a little dance. "Oh, it's lovely to be together again!" he cried.

"Never mind the Highland Fling!" snapped Jill. "There's no time to lose. Come on!"

Chapter Eight

The audience had gone home and the hall
was empty.

A crestfallen Ms Binns stood by the door
with the empty money-box in her hands and
sighed.

"Oh dear," she murmured. "All gone.
Everyone wanted their money back." As she
sighed again and turned to leave she saw
Brat Gripewater oozing towards her smarmily.

"Never mind, Ms Binns," he said smoothly. "It was a brave try. There's no pleasing everyone, is there?" His features were solemn but his lips twitched as he tried not to laugh out loud in triumph. "Remember, all is not lost. My offer to buy the playing field still stands."

"Oh, yes," said Ms Binns, distracted. "Your offer. Of course."

"Of course!" smirked Brat, and he pulled the document of sale from his inside pocket.

"If you'll just sign here," he said, pointing to the bottom of the document, "then that will be that."

Ms Binns leaned forward, pen poised.

But before she could sign there was an enormous thumping noise from the other end of the hall. Both she and Brat looked up, startled.

On to the stage stamped Bogle, tossing Ms Binns's big safe from one hand to the other as if it were an empty cardboard box.

Brat's mouth fell open and Ms Binns stared in amazement.

"That must be Mr Muscle Mountain," she whispered in disbelief. "What's he doing throwing my safe around? That thing weighs a tonne!"

Bogle stopped in the centre of the stage and grinned.

"For my next trick," he announced, "I'll balance this thing on my nose." And he did.

As Bogle put the safe down Ms Binns heard a burst of clapping from the wings. On to the stage walked Charlie Chill, followed by the other performers ... Madame Screetchowtski, Fingers O'Bone and Pharaoh McFakery.

Brat glowered angrily. Something was wrong ... he could tell.

"Ms Binns," he said urgently, "if you could just sign the document..."

Flustered, Ms Binns leaned over the papers again, but Charlie shouted, "Stop! Ms Binns! Don't sign that! Look!"

Charlie held up a big brown envelope with the words **SCHOOL FETE MONEY** printed on it.

"We found it stuffed down behind your safe, Ms Binns. It wasn't stolen after all." He pointed accusingly at Brat. "Mr Gripewater arranged for it to be hidden, so you would think it was stolen and have to sell the playing field." He led Thothage to the front of the stage. "Thoth ... I mean ... Mr McFakery overheard Brat and his men discussing it. This is the proof you wanted."

Thothage nodded and Charlie grinned. "So you see, you don't have to sell the playing field after all!"

"Oh!" cried Ms Binns, giving a little hop in delight. "How wonderful!"

"This is all nonsense!" cried Brat angrily, but the Head Teacher turned and looked at him frostily.

"Charlie warned me before about you but I didn't take any notice. But I now realize that everything's true." She gazed sternly at Brat as if he were a troublesome pupil. "You are a very, very naughty person and I will not be signing. Not now, not ever!" She handed the document back to Brat who, trembling with rage, snatched it and stormed out of the hall.

"Charlie!" cried Ms Binns as she strode towards the stage. "You have saved the day!"

"It wasn't just me, Ms Binns," replied Charlie, handing her the envelope. "It was my Aunt Jill ... and ... er ... I mean ... Madame Screetchowtski, Mr Muscle Mountain, Fingers O'Bone and Pharaoh McFakery all helped."

Ms Binns nodded to everyone.

"The concert was ... er ... unusual to say the least," she said. "And I must admit to being disappointed that it was not a success. But," she shrugged and smiled, "it doesn't matter now! All's well that ends well. Thanks for all of your help." She beamed up at them.

"Now ... why don't you all change out of your costumes, take off your make-up and join me for a cup of tea and a fairy cake?"

"Lovely," said Bogle. "Have you got any cold custard?"

Charlie's mouth fell open in horror, but to his great relief Aunt Jill shook her head.

"I'm afraid we can't stay," she said. "We have another performance tonight."

"That's right!" exclaimed McGill. "We're due back in the tunnel in ten minutes!"

"The ... Tunnel?" said Ms Binns, puzzled. "Is that a theatre?"

Jill grinned.

"You could say that," she replied, and turned to the others. "Come on, back to work!"

"Thank you all again," called the Head Teacher as they disappeared behind the curtain.

Charlie was the last to go and Ms Binns waved to him. "Your aunt was right about Mr Gripewater from the start," she called.

"Perhaps I'll get a chance to meet her one day."

Charlie smiled weakly and nodded.

"Perhaps," he replied.

Jill grinned as Charlie joined her and the others.

"If only she knew, eh Charlie?" she said and winked. "If only she knew."